MR POTTER'S PET

TAKE OFF WITH A KITE!

This lively series is designed for children who have developed reading fluency and enjoy reading complete books on their own. The stories are attractively presented with plenty of illustrations which make them satisfying and fun! A perfect follow-on from the Read Alone series.

By the same author:

GEORGE SPEAKS
THE SWOOSE

Some other Kites for you to enjoy

BONESHAKER   Paul and Emma Rogers
DUMBELLINA   Brough Girling
THE INTERGALACTIC KITCHEN
   Frank Rodgers
JASON BROWN – FROG   Len Gurd
KING KEITH AND THE JOLLY LODGER
   Kaye Umansky
MR MAJEIKA   Humphrey Carpenter
NUTS   Noel Ford
OVER THE MOON AND FAR AWAY
   Margaret Nash
SEPTIMOUSE, SUPERMOUSE!
   Ann Jungman
TOMMY NINER AND THE PLANET OF
   DANGER   Tony Bradman

DICK KING-SMITH

MR POTTER'S PET

ILLUSTRATED BY HILDA OFFEN

VIKING

VIKING

Published by the Penguin Group

Penguin Books Ltd, 27 Wrights Lane, London W8 5TZ, England
Penguin Books USA Inc., 375 Hudson Street, New York, New York 10014, USA
Penguin Books Australia Ltd, Ringwood, Victoria, Australia
Penguin Books Canada Ltd, 10 Alcorn Avenue, Toronto, Ontario, Canada
M4V 3B2
Penguin Books (NZ) Ltd, 182-190 Wairau Road, Auckland 10, New Zealand

Penguin Books Ltd, Registered Offices: Harmondsworth, Middlesex, England

First published 1994

10 9 8 7 6 5 4 3 2 1

First edition

Text copyright © Fox Busters Limited, 1994
Illustrations copyright © Hilda Offen, 1994

Filmset in Linotron Palatino 14/22 pt by
Rowland Phototypesetting Ltd, Bury St Edmunds, Suffolk
Printed and bound in Great Britain by
Butler & Tanner Ltd, Frome and London

A CIP catalogue record for this book is available from the British Library

ISBN 0-670-84256-7

1.

Ever since he was a small boy, Mr Potter had had a problem. It was not a medical problem, for he enjoyed excellent health. Nor was it a matter of money, for he had never felt the lack of it. Nor did he ever fall out with the neighbours or fall foul of the law.

What Mr Potter suffered from was an addiction.

Not to cigarettes – he didn't smoke, nor to alcohol – he didn't drink, nor to food, for though he had a good appetite, he was not greedy. Mr Potter's addiction was not at all a usual one and I doubt you would ever guess what it was. So I'll tell you.

Mr Potter had never been able to stop himself from looking into the windows of pet shops.

First as a boy, then as a youth, and finally as an adult – for he continued to live at home with his parents – he would stand and gaze, year in, year out, and wish and wish that some day he might have a pet of his own. But never once did he enter a pet shop, for his mother and father, who did not like animals, had forbidden him to do so.

Then, on Mr Potter's fiftieth birthday,
Fate took a hand.

To celebrate the occasion there was a
choice of tinned crab or pork pie for tea.
Mr Potter chose the pork pie, and it was
fortunate he did so, for his mother and
father agreed that something tasted ever
so funny about the tinned crab.

Twenty-four hours later, Mr Potter was
an orphan.

On the way home from his parents'
funeral, it just so happened that Mr
Potter had to pass his local pet shop. As
he had always done, over the years, he
stopped and stood and gazed into the
window, at the puppies and kittens, at
the rabbits and guinea-pigs, at the
budgies and canaries. "If only I could
have a pet of my own," he said wistfully,
as he had always said, over the years.

Then it suddenly dawned on him that
he could!

Who was to stop him? Thanks to the
tinned crab, no one.

Thanks to the tinned crab, he need no
longer simply stand and stare hopelessly
at the window. He could go in! He could
go in and buy himself a pet, any sort of
pet, whatever he fancied!

As a small boy, he'd always wanted a
white mouse. As he grew, so did the

animals he dreamed of owning – a gerbil, a hamster, a guinea-pig, a rabbit – until when grown up he thought how nice it would be to have a cat or a dog. But since he had never been allowed inside a pet shop, Mr Potter had never had to make a choice. Now, suddenly, he could!

He pushed open the door.

"Shut that door!" cried a loud angry voice as he entered the shop, and Mr Potter hastened to obey. He was accustomed always to do as he was bid. But I must say, he thought, that shopkeeper is a very rude fellow. How does he expect to run a successful business if he shouts at his customers in that way?

However, when Mr Potter turned round, he thought that the shopkeeper looked a polite sort of person, who smiled and said in quite a different tone,

"Good morning, sir. What can I do for you?"

"Well," said Mr Potter, "I want to buy a pet."

"For a grandchild perhaps?" said the shopkeeper.

"No. For myself."

"What sort of pet?"

Mr Potter turned to look at the cages

ranged along the walls.

"I don't know," he said, to which the reply was, "Silly fool!"

Mr Potter was a mild-mannered man who had never been known to say "Boo" to a goose. For all of his fifty years he had done exactly as he was told, by his teachers at school and, at home, by his late mother and father. Which is why he

had shut the door of the pet shop even though it seemed to him that the shopkeeper could well have said "please". But now to be called a silly fool by a perfect stranger was a bit much.

He took off his spectacles so as not to have to meet the shopkeeper's eye and polished them vigorously with his handkerchief.

"Just because I haven't yet made my mind up what sort of pet I want," he said rather nervously, "I really don't think you have any right to call me that."

The shopkeeper smiled.

"Call you what?" he said, and as if in answer the different voice said, "Silly fool!"

Putting his spectacles on again, Mr Potter saw that the speaker was sitting in a large cage hanging just above the shopkeeper's head. It was a bird the size

of a dove, glossy black in colour save for
a white bar on each wing, with yellow
feet and wattles, and a stout orange-red
bill.

"I'm sorry," said the shopkeeper.
"You're not the first person to complain
about his language by a long chalk. He's
the rudest bird in the world, he is."

"What is he?" said Mr Potter.

"He's a mynah," said the shopkeeper.
"A Greater Indian Hill-Mynah, to give

him his proper title. They live in the forests of the hilly parts of India. Wonderful mimics they are, better than any parrot, and he's as good a one as I've ever heard, but he never says a civil word to anyone."

"Shut your face!" said the mynah.

"See what I mean?" said the shopkeeper. "No wonder I haven't been able to sell him. Now then, sir, perhaps I can help you choose a pet of some sort. Do you see anything here you fancy?"

Mr Potter pottered round the shop, looking at all the different animals that were for sale. All the time he kept half an eye on the mynah, waiting to hear what it would say next, but it remained silent.

Mr Potter completed his tour of the shop and stood looking up at the bird.

"How much?" he said.

"The mynah?" said the shopkeeper.

"Yes," said Mr Potter.

"Mind your own business," said the mynah.

"Two hundred pounds," said the shopkeeper. "Which is a fair price, I assure you."

"Rubbish!" said the mynah.

"In fact," said the shopkeeper, "for two hundred pounds I'll throw in the cage as well."

"Done!" said Mr Potter.

"Silly fool!" said the mynah.

2.

At home, Mr Potter hung the cage in his parents' bedroom.

"This is *your* room from now on," he said to the mynah.

The bird turned its head this way and that, surveying its new quarters critically, first with one large liquid eye and then with the other.

"Well," said Mr Potter, "how d'you like it?"

For answer the mynah made a rude noise.

"That's not very polite," said Mr Potter. "I ask you a civil question and I expect a civil answer. What do you think of your room?"

"It's a dump," said the mynah.

Mr Potter shook his head and sighed. He could see that he would have to educate the bird, to say nice things instead of nasty ones. If he was always polite to it, surely it would learn by example?

"Pardon me for asking," he said, "but what is your name?"

"Mind your own business," said the mynah.

Mr Potter smiled bravely.

"My name's Potter," he said.

The mynah laughed loudly. It was not a nice laugh.

"Can you say that? Potter . . . Potter . . . Potter . . . Potter."

"Ah, shut up!" said the mynah.

Mr Potter picked up the telephone that stood beside his late parents' bed and dialled the number of the pet shop.

"Hallo," he said. "I bought a mynah

21

bird from you today."

"I'm sorry, sir," said the shopkeeper hastily, "but I can't possibly take him back. I've already paid your cheque into the bank."

"No, no," said Mr Potter. "That's not why I'm ringing. I simply forgot to ask you if he has a name."

"I called him a good many names,"

said the shopkeeper drily, "and so will you, I expect."

Mr Potter put down the receiver.

"That was the man at the pet shop," he said.

"Stupid old twit," said the mynah.

"Oh, I don't know. He seemed a nice chap."

"Rubbish!"

23

Mr Potter began to feel that he had made a bad bargain. He had paid a great deal of money for this, his very first pet, because he'd liked the way it could speak as clearly as any human. Now, it seemed he was condemned to putting up with its everlasting rudeness. If only it would say something reasonable. He tried again.

"Tell me, what would you like me to call you?" he said.

"Suit yourself," said the bird, and turned its back on him.

Mr Potter considered what name you could give to a bad-tempered, bad-mannered Greater Indian Hill-Mynah, and that brought into his mind the greatest of Indian hills, well, more than that, the highest mountain in the world.

"How about 'Everest'?" he said.

He waited for the mynah to say "Shut up" or "Silly fool" or "Stupid old twit", but it simply said, "OK."

The tone of its voice was dispirited, as though it didn't much care what it was called, and a sudden thought struck Mr Potter. Was the bird simply unhappy? Was this why it was always so surly?

"Look, Everest," he said, "you've got plenty of good food, mealworms and a special mynah-mixture that I bought from the pet shop, and some fresh fruit to peck at, and clean water to drink, and a handsome cage. What more do you want?"

"Use your brains," said Everest and, turning round, he began to hammer with his stout beak at the cage door.

He wants to come out, thought Mr Potter.

"You want to come out?" he said.

"You got it, Potter," said Everest.

So surprised was Mr Potter to be addressed by name that without further thought he reached up and unlatched the door of the cage.

The mynah hopped out and down on to his new owner's shoulder.

Mr Potter could see out of the corner of his eye that strong orange-red bill, and it looked very sharp. He stood stock-still,

expecting to be rewarded with a vicious peck from this grumpy bird.

Then, to his great surprise, he felt instead the gentlest of tugs at the lobe of his ear and heard the voice of his pet, sounding quite different from its usual harsh tones.

"Thanks, Potter," said Everest softly. "You're a pal."

Mr Potter positively beamed with pleasure. Living at home under the thumbs of his mother and father, he had never in all his fifty years made any friends. Now at last, it seemed, he had one! And he had found the reason for Everest's constant rudeness. All the bird wanted was a little bit of freedom, an occasional outing from the confines of his cage, a short flight around the room perhaps. No harm in that, he couldn't escape, the window was closed. Wasn't it?

Mr Potter turned his head and caught his breath. The top part of the old-fashioned sash window was a little way open, six inches maybe.

"Everest," he said.

"Yes, Potter?"

"How about popping back into your cage for a moment? There's something I've forgotten to do."

"So I see," said the mynah, and he

jumped off Mr Potter's shoulder and flew on to the top of the window frame.

For a moment Everest perched there, turning his head for one last backward look.

"Nice knowing you, Potter," he said, and was gone.

3.

All that evening Mr Potter searched for his pet.

He searched his own garden, and looked into the gardens of his neighbours, and walked all round the nearby park, crying, "Everest! Everest! Everest!" People he met looked at him askance. Those who knew him by sight thought he had become deranged by the sudden deaths of his mother and father. Those who didn't thought he was drunk.

"Everest! Everest! Where on earth are you?" he called, and an earnest-looking schoolboy took the question seriously and replied, "In the Himalayas. On the border between Nepal and Tibet." But of the mynah there was neither sight nor sound.

Darkness fell and Mr Potter went to bed and slept badly. His pet was lost. He still had the cage, of course, he could go to the pet shop and buy some other bird, but that would be cold comfort. Nothing could replace Everest, his first and only friend.

None the less he got up very early in the morning and walked to the pet shop, hoping against hope that the mynah would be sitting outside its closed door, like a homing pigeon waiting to be let into its loft. But of course it wasn't.

Mr Potter trudged despondently home again. After breakfast, he thought, I'll ring the police and I'll put advertisements everywhere and I'll offer a reward. But even if anyone saw him, how could they catch him? And supposing someone did and I got Everest back, the bird would have to be caged, for ever. Which is exactly what he hated and why he was so grumpy. At least now he's free, Mr Potter said to himself, free as a bird. So one of us is happy.

He put aside the thought of breakfast and went upstairs, nerving himself to face the empty room, the empty cage. He opened the door.

"Morning, Potter," said a muffled voice, and there, in his cage, on his

perch, was the mynah with a mouthful
of mealworms.

Mr Potter's first impulse was to rush
forward and close the window. If I can
manage to do that, he thought, then
even if I'm not quick enough to shut the
door of the cage, at least he won't be able
to get out of the room. But before he
could move, Everest swallowed the
mealworms, hopped out of the cage and
perched on the back of a chair.

"Shut the window, Potter," he said.
"There's an awful draught."

Stunned, Mr Potter obeyed.

"You're back!" he said hoarsely.

"Looks like it," said Everest.

"But . . . but why?"

"Hungry. And cold. Too many cats
about anyway. You haven't got one, I
hope?"

"No, no, you're the first pet I've ever had."

"Pet, eh? That's a bit patronizing."

"Oh sorry, the first friend, I meant to say, Everest," said Mr Potter.

"That's better," said the mynah.

He began to preen himself, stretching his wings and settling his feathers.

"About this cage, Potter," he said.

"Yes?"

"OK for sleeping in. OK for eating in. But in future, let's leave the door open. OK?"

"You mean, you want to be free to fly about the house?" said Mr Potter.

"Sure," said Everest. "No problem, is there?"

A great many problems, thought Mr Potter. He pictured the equestrian statue in the middle of the park, liberally bespattered with pigeon droppings, and imagined the state in which his house would very shortly be. But how should he put it to Everest?

At that moment the mynah finished his preening and, raising his tail, deposited a large squidgy white mess on the bedroom carpet.

"That's better," he said.

"Well, actually," said Mr Potter, "it's not."

"Oh sorry, Potter," said Everest. "I didn't think. Not used to being out of a cage. Where do you want me to do it?"

Mr Potter hesitated. Outside in the garden, I suppose, he thought. But then he might fly away again.

"Outside in the garden?" said Everest.

"But . . ." said Mr Potter.

"Worry not, pal," said Everest, flying up on to his shoulder. "East, west, home's best. But supposing it's snowing or blowing a gale or raining cats and dogs? Where do you do it, Potter?"

Dazedly Mr Potter walked to the bathroom with its old-fashioned claw-footed bath and its antiquated WC with high cistern and dangling chain and pointed to the lavatory bowl.

"In there?" said Everest.

"Yes," said Mr Potter, "and then you can get rid of it," and he pulled the plug.

Head cocked, the mynah watched the water flushing away.

"Neat," he said.

"You could, um, manage, could you?" said Mr Potter.

"No major problem there," said Everest. "Not even a mynah one. But I'm all right at the moment, thanks," and once again he nibbled at the lobe of Mr Potter's ear.

Mr Potter suddenly felt not merely very happy but very hungry.

"Come on, Everest," he said. "I haven't had any breakfast yet, and I dare say you wouldn't mind another beakful."

In the kitchen Mr Potter got out the frying-pan and cooked himself a huge fatty breakfast, just the kind his mother had never given him – bacon and eggs and mushrooms and kidneys and baked beans and black pudding and a big slice of fried bread. And he sat himself down at the head of the table where his father had always sat, with his elbows on the table, which his mother had never allowed. He had taken off his jacket and his tie, something that neither of his parents would ever have permitted, and he sat there in his shirtsleeves, shovelling the grub in like a greedy schoolboy, while the grease ran down his chin and the mynah stood on the table, nibbling at a biscuit and watching attentively.

Mr Potter cut himself another thick slice of bread and wiped all round his greasy plate. He swallowed the last mouthful and let out a loud, satisfied belch.

"Nice one, Potter," said Everest.

"Oh dear," said Mr Potter. "I beg your pardon. I was forgetting my manners."

"Worry not, pal," said Everest. "That was the mother and father of a meal you put away. Do you always eat like that?"

"Well, no," said Mr Potter. "My mother and father, you see, would not have approved. They ate very sparingly."

But, in the end, not wisely, he thought.

"Fallen off their perches, have they?" said Everest.

"Sorry?"

"Shot their bolt? Had their chips? Turned their toes up? Popped their clogs? Died?"

"Yes, very recently. Last week, in fact."

"And you've lived with them here? All your life?"

"Yes."

Everest let out a low whistle of amazement.

"Weird, Potter," he said. "Really

weird. I flew the nest the moment I got
my flight feathers.''

"They didn't want me to go," said Mr
Potter.

They didn't let me do anything I
wanted to, he thought.

"You must miss 'em," said the mynah.

"Oh yes," said Mr Potter absently,
taking a long noisy drink of the strong

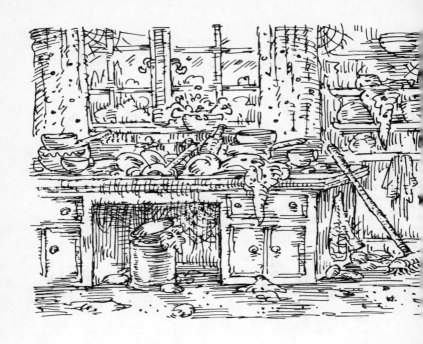

Indian tea that his parents, preferring
weak China, had never kept.

"You'll be lonely," said Everest.

"Not now," said Mr Potter. "Not now
I've got you for a friend."

Everest cast a critical eye round the
kitchen. He saw the woodlice crawling
around the floor, the spiders' webs in the
corners of the ceiling, the smeary

windows, the stack of old washing-up in
the sink, the dirty tea-cloths, the dust
everywhere.

"That's all very well, Potter," he said.
"But what you need is a girlfriend."

4.

Peggy Flower, thought Mr Potter! The
only girlfriend I ever had.

At least that's how I thought of her,
though I never told her how I felt. She
was small and rather plump with fair
hair, I can see her now. Though we were
the same age, we were in different
classes, but I would watch her in the
playground, skipping about with some of
the other girls, and she smiled at me,
once.

"Penny for your thoughts, Potter,"
said Everest, his head cocked on one
side.

A silly idea came into Mr Potter's
mind, which was that when he looked at
him like that, the bird could actually read

his thoughts, never mind offering a
penny for them.

"I did have a girlfriend, Everest," he
said.

"Turned you down, did she?" said the
mynah.

"No."

"Why didn't you marry her then?"

"We were only ten," said Mr Potter. "She moved away. I've never seen her since."

"Pity," said Everest. "I tell you straight, Potter, this place needs a woman's touch. It's a tip! What you need is a housekeeper."

"Oh no," said Mr Potter.

"What's the matter?" said Everest. "Can't afford it?"

"It isn't that," said Mr Potter, and indeed it wasn't, for thanks to that tin of crab he was now so well off that he had even been able to give up the job that had bored him stiff for thirty years.

But to have a strange woman living in my house, he thought – I couldn't bear that. Women had always made him feel shy. Anyway, he had never met a female that he liked. Apart from Peggy Flower.

"Oh no," he said. "I'll manage."

46

"We'll see," said Everest.

And over the coming weeks they saw.

Never before had Mr Potter realized
the meaning of housework. Now he
found it never-ending. Quite apart from
tidying the place up and trying to keep it
tidy, there was the shopping and the
cooking and the washing and the ironing

and the mending. There was silver to be polished and brass to be burnished and windows to be cleaned – the list was endless. So it was that in due course an advertisement appeared in the local newspaper.

Respectable bachelor, 50, non-smoker, sober, simple tastes, requires live-in house-keeper. Generous wages, holidays for suit-able applicant. Own comfortable quarters. *Apply* Mr Peter Potter, The Laurels, Green-field Avenue.

The very next morning there was a loud knock at the door.

Mr Potter paled.

"Oh Everest," he said. "What if she's not suitable?"

"Leave that to me," said Everest. "You give me a sign and I'll do the rest."

"What sort of sign?"

"Scratch your bald spot."

The moment he opened the door, Mr
Potter knew he was not going to like the
large jolly woman who thrust out a hand
that gripped his own like a vice.

"We'll soon have this place to rights,"
she boomed as he showed her round. "I
can see we're going to get on like a house
on fire, ha, ha, not a happy choice of
words, eh?"

Not a happy choice of housekeeper,
thought Mr Potter and he looked wildly
round for Everest, but the mynah was
nowhere to be seen.

"I'll start next week then, Mr Potter,"

said the large jolly woman.

Oh, what shall I do, thought Mr
Potter? What can I say? Where's Everest?
He scratched his bald spot like mad.

"That's agreed then," said the woman,
and Mr Potter opened his mouth, to say
he knew not what. At that instant he
heard the sound of his own voice,
coming from somewhere just behind his
head.

"No, it isn't," said his voice. "I wouldn't employ you if you were the last person on earth. And now get lost, you silly great cow."

As the front door banged furiously behind the outraged woman, Everest emerged from his hiding-place.

"Neat, eh, Potter?" he said in his normal harsh tones.

"You were brilliant," said Mr Potter. "Just when I thought she had me cornered."

"Worry not, pal," said Everest. "We need to find the right person. Better luck next time, maybe."

The next applicant arrived that afternoon. In contrast to the first one, she was softly spoken and daintily dressed, and her hand, as Mr Potter greeted her, felt soft and lingered in his long enough to make him uncomfortable.

Everything about her was lady-like. Her
voice was carefully genteel, and she
constantly fluttered her eyelashes at Mr
Potter with a roguish smile.

After their tour of the house, she stood
very close to him in the sitting-room, in

front of a bookshelf in which Everest was crouching, and the sight of that lady-like bottom was too much for the mynah.

"Oh! Mr Potter!" squealed the would-be housekeeper happily. "You are naughty!"

"Naughty?" said Mr Potter, puzzled.

"Pinching a girl's sit-upon! I can see we're going to have lots of fun!"

Once again Mr Potter scratched his bald spot with a will, and once again, as he prepared to reply, he heard his own voice.

"Not on your nelly!" it said. "Mutton dressed as lamb doesn't interest me, so go and make sheep's eyes at someone else, you old bag."

"I couldn't resist it," said Everest when the front door had banged again. "Just a couple of little tweaks, that's all."

Mr Potter mopped his eyes.

"Oh dear!" he said. "What a laugh! But I'm still no nearer getting a housekeeper."

The telephone rang.

"Yes?" said Mr Potter. "Yes, that's right. No, the position isn't filled. This evening at seven? Yes, that's quite convenient. Goodbye."

He turned to the mynah.

"She sounded all right," he said.

"Third time lucky?" said Everest.

5.

As seven o'clock approached, Mr Potter found himself becoming increasingly nervous. The way that Everest had disposed of the first two applicants was all very well, but he did hope that this time he would not have to call upon the bird for help.

It was not in his nature to be rude or unkind to people, and already he felt guilty that those two women had been so treated.

"Everest," he said.

"Yes, Potter?"

"If this one's no good, do you think you could let her off a bit more lightly? Be a bit more polite, I mean?"

The mynah put his head on one side.

"Feeling guilty, huh?" he said.

"Yes."

"Suit yourself," said Everest. "In fact,
why not tell her yourself? If you don't
like the look of her, all you have to do is
say, 'I will let you know my decision
later'."

"All right," said Mr Potter.

He looked at his watch.

"Do you need to go outside?" he asked.

"Too dark," said Everest. "Owls and pussy-cats out there. I'll pop up to the bathroom."

"Better pull the plug," he said when he returned, and no sooner had Mr Potter obeyed than there was a knock on the front door.

The first thing Mr Potter noticed as he opened it was that this woman had a particularly nice smile.

She was middle-aged, of below average height and comfortably rounded, and her handshake was neither fierce nor flabby but firm.

She had good things to say about the house as Mr Potter showed her round, and sensible suggestions to make, and she seemed most understanding as he told her of the loss of his parents and of the problems that he now faced. Mr Potter found that he was not at all shy with her. It was almost as though they were old friends.

"Shall I make a pot of tea?" he said when they had finished their tour.

"Please," she said, "can't I make it for you?"

"No, no," said Mr Potter, thinking how nice it would be to have his tea made and brought to him by this pleasant person.

"Indian or China?" he said.

"Indian, please," said the pleasant person. "And strong enough to stand the spoon up in!"

"Oh good!" said Mr Potter. "That's the way I like it. By the way, I didn't catch your name?"

"It's Margaret."

"I noticed a birdcage," said Margaret
as they were sitting drinking their tea,
"in that big bedroom that used to be
your parents'."

"Ah yes," said Mr Potter. "I should
have told you. I do have a pet."

"Really?" said Margaret. "What sort?"

At that precise moment Everest, who
had been listening outside the door,

hopped into the room and straight up on to the arm of her chair.

"Oh!" she cried. "How lovely! A Greater Indian Hill-Mynah!" and she stretched out her hand and began gently to stroke Everest down the length of his glossy black back.

Any doubts that Mr Potter had ever had about the wisdom of employing a housekeeper vanished at that instant, and at the same time he knew beyond doubt that this was the person for the job.

"His name's Everest," he said. "You would be working for both of us."

Margaret smiled that nice smile.

"You don't recognize me, do you?" she said.

Recognize her, thought Mr Potter, why on earth should I? and in his puzzlement he raised a hand and scratched his bald

spot. As he did so, he saw Everest
watching him, head on one side.

"NO!" he said loudly.

"You mean, you don't recognize me?"

"Oh sorry," said Mr Potter. "I was
talking to Everest. I thought he might be
going to say something."

"Is he a good talker?"

"Worry not, pal," said Everest to Mr

Potter. "I read you. Like a book."

Margaret almost dropped her teacup.

"What an absolutely amazing bird!" she said. "He doesn't just talk. He makes sense. What else does he say?"

"Anything you like, miss," said Everest, "so long as it's in plain English."

"And in plain English," said Mr

Potter, "the job is yours. If you want it."

"Oh, I do," said Margaret, "and thank you. But I can see you're still wondering who I am, so I'd better put you out of your misery, Peter."

"How do you know my name?" said Mr Potter.

"It was in the advertisement, wasn't it? Can it be the same Peter Potter, I said to myself? I've only just moved back to these parts, you see. I was working up north and I was made redundant. So I thought I'd like to come back and look for a job in the town where I was born. And I'm so glad I did. But I haven't told you my surname, have I, Peter? It's Flower."

"Flower!" cried Mr Potter and now it was his turn almost to drop his cup. He stared at the figure sitting opposite him, small and rather plump with fair hair

now peppered with grey, and suddenly
he was watching Peggy Flower skipping
about in the playground with some of
the other girls as forty years vanished
without trace.

"But she wasn't called Margaret," he
said.

"Oh yes, she was," said his new
housekeeper. "Peggy for short."

6.

With the coming of Peggy Flower, life at the Laurels changed completely. After a couple of months, Mr Potter had almost forgotten how dark and dingy the place had been all his life. Now there was bright fresh paint everywhere, his own handiwork, what's more. Room by room, he had redecorated the entire house, while Peggy re-organized it, and Everest flew between them, carrying messages from one to the other.

"Peggy says do you want some coffee?" he might say to the painter, or to the housekeeper, "Potter says isn't it lunchtime yet?"

Mr Potter now occupied his parents' old room.

"It's the nicest bedroom in the house, Peter," said Peggy, "as well as being the biggest. I shall be perfectly happy in your old room, and Everest, you could have the smaller of the spare rooms, couldn't you? It's handy for the bathroom and it overlooks the back garden. Not far for you to go, either way. Would that be OK?"

"Worry not, Peg," said Everest, and he treated her ear to a nibble.

Altogether the three of them were very content with each other's company. No thought crossed their minds that anything might happen to upset the even tenor of their days and ways. But it did.

One morning Peggy returned from shopping to find Mr Potter in a right old state.

"Oh, I'm so glad you're back!" he cried as she came into the kitchen. "Everest

has had an accident! Look!'' and there on
the table lay the still body of Mr Potter's
pet.

''What happened?'' said his
housekeeper.

''He flew upstairs to go to the
bathroom,'' said Mr Potter, ''and after a
while I thought he's been gone a long
time, and I went upstairs and there he
was on the floor. The seat-cover of the
lavatory was down. It must have fallen

and hit him on the head. I think he's dead."

Peggy Flower picked up the mynah and held him in her hands.

"No, he isn't," she said. "I can feel his heart beating," and quickly she emptied her shopping-basket and laid Everest in it, wrapped in a teacloth.

"Off you go to the vet," she said, "and try not to worry. I'm sure he'll be all right."

"Will he be all right?" said Mr Potter anxiously to the vet. "I think he's had a bang on the head."

"How did it happen?" said the vet.

"I'm, er, not sure," said Mr Potter. "I haven't been able to ask him, you see."

The vet raised his eyebrows.

"Answers questions, does he?" he said.

Mr Potter smiled nervously. If he only

knew, he thought. He watched as the vet carefully examined the mynah.

"Flew into a plate-glass window, I suppose, that's the usual thing," the vet said. "Stupid bird. What's his name?"

"Everest," said Mr Potter.

"Everest, eh!" said the vet with a grin. "Well, I tell you what, he's bumped his summit on summat! But I don't think he's cracked his skull, so we mustn't make mountains out of molehills, eh?"

At this point the mynah opened one eye.

"Oh Everest!" cried Mr Potter. "Speak to me!"

Everest opened the other eye.

"Say something – anything!"

"Who's a pretty boy then?" said the vet.

Everest remained silent.

"He's lost for words," said the vet

drily. "But I can't find much wrong with
him. Take him away and keep him warm
– inside as well as out."

"Inside?" said Mr Potter.

"Yes. Give him a drop of something,
to help him get over the shock. Brandy
will do."

71

"A drop of brandy," said Mr Potter
when he arrived home.

"For you?" said Peggy, producing a
bottle from the larder.

"No, for Everest."

"He's all right?"

"He's conscious."

"Has he spoken?"

"Not a word."

"And nor would you," said Everest
weakly, "if you had a headache like
mine."

Mr Potter and Miss Flower looked at
one another over the shopping-basket,
and their eyes shone, with relief and joy.

Carefully, Peggy filled an egg spoon.

"Now then, Everest," she said,
"would you like a little drink?" and as
the mynah opened his beak to reply, she
tipped the brandy down him.

"Nice?" said Mr Potter.

"Better?" said Peggy.

"Yes," said Everest in a voice that was already a good deal stronger. "How about the other half?"

"We'll have one too, shall we?" said Mr Potter to his housekeeper, and to his pet, "Here's to a complete recovery. Your health, Everest!"

"Cheers," said Peggy.

"Down the hatch!" said Everest.

"Now then," said Mr Potter, "you have a good sleep and you'll wake up feeling a new bird."

"Everesht by name, Everesht by nature," said the mynah.

"What do you mean?"

"I feel pretty high," said Mr Potter's pet. He gave a squawk of laughter. "Worry not, palsh," he said. "Let'sh all have one for the road."

7.

For the rest of that day Everest slept. He appeared at breakfast next morning in a distinctly grumpy frame of mind.

"Rice Krispies, Everest?" said Peggy.

These were the mynah's favourites because of the sounds they made.

"No," said Everest. "They're too noisy. My head's bursting."

"Haven't lost your headache then?" said Mr Potter.

"Lost one, found another," said Everest.

"Don't you want anything for breakfast then?"

"Yes."

"What?"

"An aspirin."

For the rest of the day the Laurels was
unnaturally quiet as Everest sat silent in
his cage. Mr Potter attended to the seat-
cover of the lavatory, ensuring that it
would not fall again, and Peggy went to
the pet shop for fresh mealworms and to
the greengrocer for Everest's favourite
fruit, black grapes.

Tempted by these, the mynah made a hearty supper and his spirits revived. When the others had finished Mr Potter, as always, offered to help with the washing-up, and, as always, was told to go and sit down in his comfortable armchair.

In the kitchen Everest perched on the plate-rack watching the housekeeper at the sink.

"Why won't you let Potter help you?" he said.

Peggy laughed.

"Because I'm paid to help him," she said.

Everest considered this.

"Suppose you were married to him," he said, "then he'd be expected to help you."

Despite herself, Miss Flower blushed.

"Oh, get along with you!" she said,

and she flapped the dishcloth at him.

Everest flew to the sitting-room and perched on the arm of Mr Potter's chair.

"You ever been married, Potter?" he said.

"Oh no," said Mr Potter.

"Your mum and dad wouldn't let you, huh?"

It wasn't that, thought Mr Potter, though it might have been.

"No," he said. "I just never met anyone I wanted to marry."

Except one person, he said to himself, and his face grew red.

Everest cocked his head on one side in that mind-reading fashion and Mr Potter took refuge behind his newspaper.

In the still of the night Everest perched in his cage, thinking long and hard.

"It's the perfect match," he said at last softly. "They're just right for each other. But she can't very well make the first move. And he's too shy. There's only one way out. I'll have to fix it."

He lost no time about it.

The very next morning he flew in from

the garden, where Mr Potter was doing
some weeding, to the kitchen, where
Peggy was baking.

"Message from Potter," he said.

"What is it?" said Peggy.

"He says – will you marry him?" said
Everest, and off he went back to the
garden.

"Message from Peggy," he said to Mr
Potter.

"What is it?"

"She says – will you marry her?" said Everest, and he flew away to the kitchen again.

"Well?" he said.

"Oh yes!!" said Peggy.

Back went the mynah to the garden.

"Well?" he said.

"Oh yes!!" said Mr Potter.

"Well, don't just stand there, Potter," said Everest. "Get on with it."

As Mr Potter walked dazedly up the garden path, he saw Peggy Flower looking at him out of the kitchen window. She was smiling at him just as she had in the playground, all those years ago.

As if in a dream, he made his way to the kitchen, and went towards her, his muddy hands outstretched, and she took them in her floury ones, and they stood, speechless, smiling at one another.

"Come on, Potter," said a harsh voice from the doorway. "You may kiss the housekeeper."

So Mr Potter did.

8.

Before long Everest began to regret his matchmaking.

So wrapped up in each other were the engaged couple that they paid much less attention to Mr Potter's pet. Everest's beak was out of joint.

"Pair of blooming love-birds," he muttered sulkily. "Billing and cooing from morning till night. I might as well be stuffed for all the notice they take of me nowadays," and he flew out and perched in the top of a tall tree in a huff.

In the garden below Mr Potter and Peggy sat side by side on a rustic seat, holding hands.

"Dearest," said Mr Potter. "What would you like for a wedding present?"

83

"Another ring," said Peggy, for he had already bought her a handsome engagement ring. "A plain gold one. That's all I want."

"No, as well as that, I mean," said Mr Potter. "There must be something you've always wanted, isn't there?"

"Funnily enough," said Peggy, "there is. Just like you, Peter, I've always longed for a pet of my own, but I could never have a dog, for instance, because I was always out at work."

"I'll buy you a puppy," said Mr Potter.

"No, that's not what I would like."

"What then?"

Peggy whispered in Mr Potter's ear.

"You're joking!" he said.

"No, I'm not."

"It may take ages to get one of those."

"I don't mind waiting."

"Right," said Mr Potter, "I'll ring up

that chap at the pet shop straightaway."

In fact, it was not until after the
wedding that Mrs Potter's present
arrived at the Laurels.

One day Mr Potter came home
carrying a cardboard box. Cautiously he
opened the lid a little way, and they
peeked in.

"Oh, isn't she lovely!" cried Peggy.
"Thank you, Peter, dear!" and she gave
her new husband a kiss.

"Now then," he said. "Where's
Everest?"

"Sitting up in his tree."

"Right, let's get everything fixed up."

So it was that, ten minutes later, Everest, hearing his name called, came flying in through the kitchen window. He looked at the Potters and saw that they were both grinning broadly. He put his head on one side.

"What's up?" he said.

"Listen, Everest," said Mr Potter. "Peggy and I just wanted to say we're sorry if we seem to have been neglecting you lately, what with the wedding and everything."

"Worry not, pal," said Everest flatly.

"But we do worry," said Peggy, "and I do hope that you won't object to my new pet."

"Your new pet?" said Everest. "Not a cat?"

"No, no," they said.

"Hop up on my shoulder, old chap," said Mr Potter, "and we'll go up to your room."

"My room?" said Everest. "You've put some new animal in my room?"

"Yes, yes," they said, and they opened the door of Everest's little bedroom.

There, in his cage, was a bird the size of a dove, glossy black in colour save for a white bar on each wing, with yellow feet and wattles, and a stout orange-red bill.

The Potters stood side by side before the cage.

'Meet Peggy's new pet," said Mr Potter.

"My mynah," said Peggy.

Everest said nothing.

Instead he nibbled gently at Mr Potter's ear.

Then he hopped across and nibbled at Mrs Potter's ear.

Then he hopped back and fixed the newcomer with a long slow stare. He let out a long low wolf-whistle.

"She's beautiful, isn't she?" said Peggy.

"You said it," replied Everest.

"She doesn't say much," said Mr Potter.

"She will," replied Everest.

"You'll teach her?"

"Worry not, Potter," said Everest. "I'll teach her a thing or two."

"Oh Peter," sighed Peggy. "She's the nicest wedding present anyone ever had."

"I'm so glad you're pleased," said Mr Potter.

"I certainly am," said Mrs Potter.

"Me too," said Mr Potter's pet.